THE AWAKE SECRET

GURISHA SINGH

Copyright © Gurisha Singh
All Rights Reserved.

ISBN 979-888546203-7

This book has been published with all efforts taken to make the material error-free after the consent of the author. However, the author and the publisher do not assume and hereby disclaim any liability to any party for any loss, damage, or disruption caused by errors or omissions, whether such errors or omissions result from negligence, accident, or any other cause.

While every effort has been made to avoid any mistake or omission, this publication is being sold on the condition and understanding that neither the author nor the publishers or printers would be liable in any manner to any person by reason of any mistake or omission in this publication or for any action taken or omitted to be taken or advice rendered or accepted on the basis of this work. For any defect in printing or binding the publishers will be liable only to replace the defective copy by another copy of this work then available.

I'm thankful for being able to write this book. I would like to express my gratitude towards Norlights for encouraging me take on this project and my parents and friends for supporting me throughout and during every step.

Contents

Prologue

Keeping a secret can be tricky, no doubt. But letting it out into the world without your knowledge is way trickier and more dangerous. 'The Awake Secret' is that secret which Quinton, the new mysterious guy in the town of Bernet holds but it changes more than his life. He wasn't sure whether to let anyone in on it until Cierra. It's a turning point to whole lot of emotions, confusion and risk, which Cierra and Quinton never saw coming.

I

The Town of Bernet

Quinton Mello was known for being the quietest fellow in the town of Bernet. Most of the students at Gregor's High School used to think that it was because he just shifted to London six months ago, he was probably shy.

It's not like we never tried talking to him at school, but he always had that very intense or stern look that would drive everyone away. He used to sit in the dark corner by the window of the classroom on the last bench with his head down always. Even though everyone loved the last bench, no one messed with him for his seat. He for sure had a very different vibe.

Another cherry on top of the cake was, that he got into a major fight with a student just three days after he arrived. Now even the parents of the town were against him. However, no one knew, where his house was or where his parents lived.

When this fight got famous, I still remember, my parents sat down with me right before dinner to have a very serious discussion and to warn me about Quinton.

Although it didn't make much of a difference to me as I never even tried to talk to him. I wanted to but I always felt like he would give me a really rude reply, so I just stayed quiet.

One day, I was walking back from school, listening to my playlist and enjoying my favorite sandwich, when I saw someone was about to walk right in front of a car, and my instant thought was "Why do people take such risks in life", when I realized that it was not just someone but Quinton.

II

Hey Rude Boy!

I panicked and dropped my sandwich. I instantly shouted "Quinton, look out", nearly scratching my throat.

Quinton got startled and ducked towards the footpath. Luckily, he was saved and the car went by. I can't even explain how relieved I was that he was fine. I ran upto him kind of expecting a little thank you but instead he began shouting at me Infront of everyone.

"Cierra did you just see what you did there, just because of you that car would have crashed into me today. I can't believe you wanted me to get hurt." And he just walked away after shouting this.

In that whole speech of two minutes, I couldn't even get a chance to utter even a single word. I was so angry at him. I came back home, slammed my door, sat on my bed and just couldn't stop thinking about how angry I was.

I always knew he would be rude and but I never expected THAT.

That night, when I went down for dinner, I heard my dad talking to my mom, "That boy Quinton, who's in Cierra's class, just got saved today, I heard he was about to get in an accident, poor child.", I just kept listening to all of this, my parents feeling sad for him but decided to stay quiet. Without any delay, this incident got extremely famous in the whole town but who would tell them that I was the actual hero there.

I went upto my room later and began writing in my diary. That was honestly the best part of my day, just sitting down at night with a cup of coffee and writing about how my day went. Although today's entry was for sure going to be a very furious one.

Next morning, I woke up, got dressed and left for school. On the way, I made up my mind to atleast say SOMETHING to Quinton this time. It's not at all fair that he gets to shout at me for just for saving him and I can't even say anything. As soon as I entered the classroom, my eyes went straight towards the last bench AND.... Of course he was not there.

III

Not Fair

This made me even more angry, but I sat down on my desk with my books open. Mr. Rechmond began with the English lesson. After a minute, the whole class got interrupted by the opening of the door, and it was none other than Quinton. Arriving late as expected.

"I'm sorry", Quinton said under his breath and started walking towards his seat when Mr. Rechmond stopped him and said angrily "Quinton you are already way behind in your lessons, go and sit with Cierra for now". NO, that was my exact expression, why is this happening to me, why not anyone else.

Quinton without any delay came and sat with me. I stayed quiet the whole class and so did he, although he did fall asleep for fifteen minutes but why should I care right. As soon as the bell rang, I gathered up all the courage and was finally ready to say something to him but when I was about to, there was a sudden announcement.

"Ms. Cierra and Mr. Quinton please see me in my office right now", announced the headmaster.

Being called to the headmaster's office has always been my biggest fear and today I'd have to face that.

"I'll meet you there", Quinton said suddenly in such a calm voice as if headmaster's office was no big deal and without waiting for me to reply, he left.

I also stood up and went to the office. And here we were, both of us right in front of the headmaster's desk.

When the headmaster adjusted his glasses and began, "Ms. Cierra, you have always been one of our top graders and since Mr. Quinton's the new one here, I want you to work with him and help him in getting this year's school stall ready".

IV

Work! Work! Work!

What did I just hear, him and I working together, no way. Well, that's what I said in my head.

"Sure" That's all I was able to say to the headmaster though. Quinton said nothing. Both of us left the office at once, Quinton was about to go in the other direction when I said, "You like it or not, you'll have to help".

He just stood there quietly looking at me. I told him to come to the crafts room after one hour and went away without another word. This was turning out to be the worst day ever, why do I always get stuck in these things.

An hour later, he was already waiting in front of the door to the crafts room. He waved a little but I stayed put and without even a hi, I explained him what the school stall was and we began working.

It had already been forty something minutes of working in silence, but now I just couldn't control my anger and blurted out, "You know what, that was really rude of you to shout at me the other day."

He just dropped everything he was doing and looked at me, still not saying anything, "I just tried to save you, atleast a thank you would have been okay. You had no right to be rude to me.", I said frustrated. He still stayed quiet.

He turned around and picked up what he was doing. Then I too began working without saying anything else. Why did I just say that, that's all I was able to think about at the moment.

"I guess.... I didn't realise.", he said, after ten minutes. He didn't even look up and kept working. What does he mean by 'I guess'. Anyways, this time I stayed quiet.

Atleast now we were talking a bit, be it for work only. We managed to complete the stall and the posters right before the Christmas fest. It took us nearly two weeks. But even after that, we both were not on very good terms. That apart, it was time to finally present our work.

V

Merry Christmas

On the morning of the Annual Christmas fest, we both came to school very early to set up the whole thing. Gregor's High was certainly very proud of this event.

As soon as we were done setting up, the headmaster came and stood in front of our stall, gazing at it for atleast a minute.

"You two have done a fine work" said the headmaster and left. Well, that was a high praise from him. Within an hour the event started. Throughout the day, many students visted our stall, we didn't even have a second to rest. But that whole time, I didn't even care about Quinton.

Finally, the whole event was coming to an end, I was really tired and Quinton would have been too, he was working the same as me. I got two cups of coffee for us when he suddenly said,

"I want to show you a place, would you..... come with me?"

"What place?", I asked, surprised. "Just trust me, everything will become clear to you." He said in a very low voice.

Before I could say yes or no, he took a pen and wrote an address on a piece of paper with the time 6 PM mentioned on it and left it on the table before leaving. I looked around for a minute and then took the paper with me back home.

I had no idea about this address and had never even heard of it. I wasn't even sure whether to go or not, still I got ready and after overthinking for three hours, I went for it.

That address took me to an abandoned building back in the jungles of the town.

VI

Is This Right?

It was 6:05 at the time. I was standing outside the building, it was very cold that evening, Quinton was nowhere around. Probably it was a prank, why did I even listen to him, I should have stayed at home only.

Suddenly, someone patted on my back, I turned around and there he was, "Glad you came," he said.

I didn't even know what to say so I just nodded. Should I go inside the building? Should I leave? Should I trust him? What is this place?

So many thoughts were there in my head still I continued walking. As soon as I entered, it was very dark but the building was huge. This abandoned building at some point belonged to a very rich king maybe that's why. Anyways, from a distance, I could see some light.

A boy came running towards us. I was not expecting anyone in the building to be honest. Still, I just kept my calm face on.

That boy gave Quinton a piece of paper and he wrote a word under the secret column.

Right in the middle of the building, there were five people sitting on a table with a flickering candle.

When one of them shouted, "Hey Mello, where have you been?". Then he looked at me and suddenly became quiet. An awkward silence fell in the room when suddenly Quinton said, "Hey fellas, meet Cierra, she's a friend of mine. And Cierra, these are my friends who I've met over the years."

"It's good to meet you" I said cautiously, and they gave me a polite smile. I sat down with them. Two of them were girls and others were boys. There was definitely a sense of

awkwardness when one of the girls said, "Hi, I'm Altea."

As soon as she said this, all the others began laughing until one said, "As if that's her real name."

My expression changed into a confused one within a second's time. What did he mean by that?

Slowly everyone became kind of free and got to know each other and it was fascinating to hear the things they have went through. They really were different, their lives were not the same as other high schoolers. It didn't even realise how fast time went by. After a while, we decided to leave.

But before leaving, Altea came to me and said, "Hey, do us a favor, don't tell anyone anything that you saw here." And just left.

Again, the paper was handed out to Quinton to write the secret word which he did. One thing I can tell for sure is that the word was definitely not in English. After that we both left the building as well.

VII

Just Don't

It was around eight at the time, we both started walking through the jungles quietly. After a while I said, "What was that?" completely confused and curious.

"What do you mean, those were my friends and I just wanted you to meet them." He said in a calm voice, obviously this was not weird for him, but I had SO many questions.

"But Altea told me not to tell anyone about this meet, what was that all about?" I asked again. Quinton stopped and said "Yes, don't. Keep this to yourself. And whatever names you heard in there were not real, so please don't mention this to anyone." He said in a very serious tone as if we were on a very serious mission.

I again became quiet and we both continued walking. However, my mind was still not in the right place. We were just about to reach my home.

"Can I ask you one last question?" I asked. He nodded.

"Why did you take me to meet your friends?"

"Just to make things a bit clearer to you. You got mad at me and for some reason it made me realise you should see this." He spoke.

The explanation was still a little vague for me but well let it be, I was too tired to know more or in fact even to talk. That night I had so much to write in my diary but no energy, so I decided to sleep. Who knew this mysterious guy had such a different life.

Sleeping that night got a little difficult, for some reason, I was happy to go to school tomorrow or rather excited. Things would be changed tomorrow, right?

VIII

Everyone Knows

Same as every day, I barely dragged myself out of bed, got ready and went down for breakfast. I had this relieved feeling in my mind today. It was definitely going to be a happy day, I thought. At the dining table, I saw my parents looking at the newspaper completely shocked.

"Did something happen, you look tense?" I asked and they handed me the newspaper, the headline said, "School children found entering and breaking into an abandoned building" with a picture of Quinton near the building.

I just couldn't move right now, what was that, how did anyone know Quinton was there or about the building. I left everything and rushed to school immediately.

As soon as I was about the enter the classroom, someone pulled me aside. It was Quinton, "Oh, I was looking for you only" I said catching my breath.

"How can you do this to me, I thought you were my friend. You just told the whole town about our secret club, I trusted you with it and now I can't even believe you for a second.", he was so angry, his face became red, which was totally justified.

"But I didn't even- "I tried to explain him that it wasn't me, but he refused to listen and after a very cold stare he went away.

I didn't know what to do, who to talk to, how to tell him that it wasn't me. Everything was falling apart in my mind.

I somehow managed to sit in class, Quinton was not in the class for any lesson that day, I kept waiting and waiting. I came back home, yet I couldn't rest even for a bit. I just wanted to go to school next day and explain everything to him, that this was just a misunderstanding.

IX
Talk Please

Next day I rushed to school very early, ran upto my class looking for Quinton, he still wasn't there.

It had been a week now since I had seen him. I wanted to but he was not attending school. That day I decided to go to the headmaster. I had to know where he was or where he lived.

"Yes, Ms. Cierra, how may I help you?", the headmaster asked.

"Actually, my classmate Quinton has not been attending his classes, I just wanted to know where he is?" I asked, concerned.

"Oh, I think you don't know, but Mr. Quinton left Gregor's High last week itself", headmaster said.

What, I was so disappointed right now. I felt really guilty like everything was my fault but I didn't even say anything. What was I supposed to do now. After school that day, I was going back home, but for some reason I just changed my route went to that same abandoned building. It looked really different in broad daylight.

I entered and it was completely empty, though I was expecting him to be here. Still, I walked towards that table, all the memories of that evening rushing back. The place looked so big right now. Then I saw something on the table, it was note, I picked it up and read,

To Cierra,

" The memories of that moon,

Makes me believe I'll see you soon.

I'll always be here, just not sure where.

And I know it wasn't you,

As in our group, you never were new."

- *Quinton*

I took that note with me put it in my pocket, and left the building immediately. I was not expecting myself to be that calm after reading it as I was now. Why? No one knows.

I just couldn't believe he wasn't there and after that day I never went back there because I would not be able to handle it.

X

It's All New

It has been five months since the whole life changing incident, I have been focusing on my studies since then, still kind of dealing with the fact that things have changed now... A LOT.

Complicated life used to be a joke for me some time ago, but not this time. I always kept that note from Quinton stuck to my bedroom wall, I just couldn't afford losing it.

And I haven't seen or talked about that building ever since, and never found those friends of Quinton but I feel I'm fine without all of it. To be honest I always wanted to live that night again when I first went to the building. The saddest part is that day's diary entry is still a blank page.

Though one good thing was, even though Quinton wasn't there anymore, still everyone kept his seat empty in the class.

It's funny how just one event in your life can completely change everything and you never know when that'll be, but I guess that's the way life is.

About The Author

Gurisha Singh is passionate writer, who loves to read and believes in the power of words. Someone who sees each project as a new learning experience. It's a dream come true to be able to have a whole book.

Printed by Libri Plureos GmbH in Hamburg, Germany